*To the Forty-Niners,
and the picture you are creating together*

—S.D.R.

*For my father, Herb,
who always kept plenty of crayons around*

—M.L.

Printed in the United States by Random House, Inc., New York,
and simultaneously in Canada by Random House of Canada Limited, Toronto.

http://www.randomhouse.com/

Library of Congress Cataloging-in-Publication Data:
DeRolf, Shane. The crayon box that talked / by Shane DeRolf
illustrated by Michael Letzig.   p. cm.
SUMMARY: Although they are many different colors, the crayons in a box
discover that when they get together they can appreciate each
other and make a complete picture.
ISBN 0-679-88611-7 (trade)
(1. Crayons—Fiction.   2. Color—Fiction.
3. Individuality—Fiction.   4. Stories in rhyme.)
I. Letzig, Michael, ill. II. Title. PZ8.3.D4465Cr 1997 (E)–dc21 97-19092

Printed in the United States of America
10 9

The Crayon Box that Talked

by Shane DeRolf

illustrated by Michael Letzig

Random House 🏠 New York

While walking in a toy store,
The day before today...

I overheard a crayon box,
With many things to say.

"I don't like Red!" said Yellow,
And Green said, "Nor do I!
And no one here likes Orange,
But no one knows just why."

"We are a box of crayons
That doesn't get along."
Said Blue to all the others,
"Something here is wrong!"

Well, I bought that box of crayons,

And took it home with me,

And laid out all the colors
So the crayons could all see...

They watched me as I colored,
With Red and Blue and Green,
And Black and White and Orange,
And every color in between.

They watched as Green became the grass
And Blue became the sky.
The Yellow sun was shining bright
On White clouds drifting by.

Colors changing as they touched,
Becoming something new.
They watched me as I colored.
They watched till I was through.

And when I'd finally finished,
I began to walk away.
And as I did, the crayon box
Had something more to say…

"I do like Red!" said Yellow.
And Green said, "So do I!
And, Blue, you were terrific,
So high up in the sky!"

"We are a box of crayons,
Each one of us unique.
But when we get together…

The picture is complete."

YUM YUM!